The S

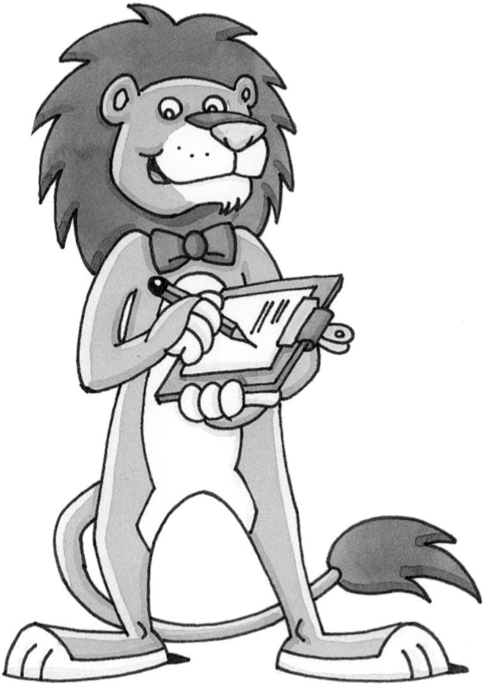

Illustrated by Kelvin Hawley

Rigby

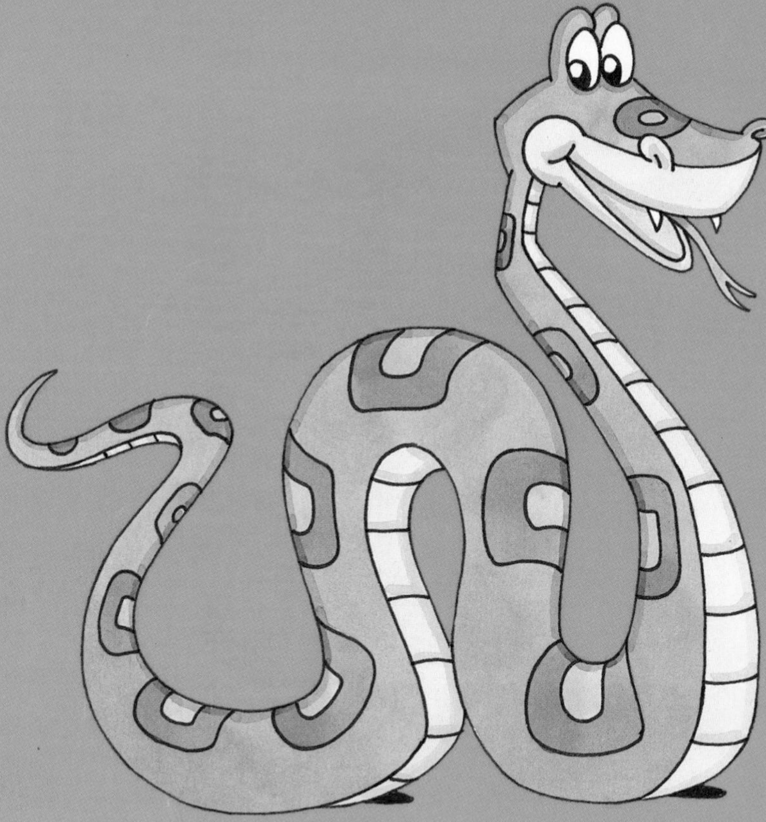

Here is a snake.

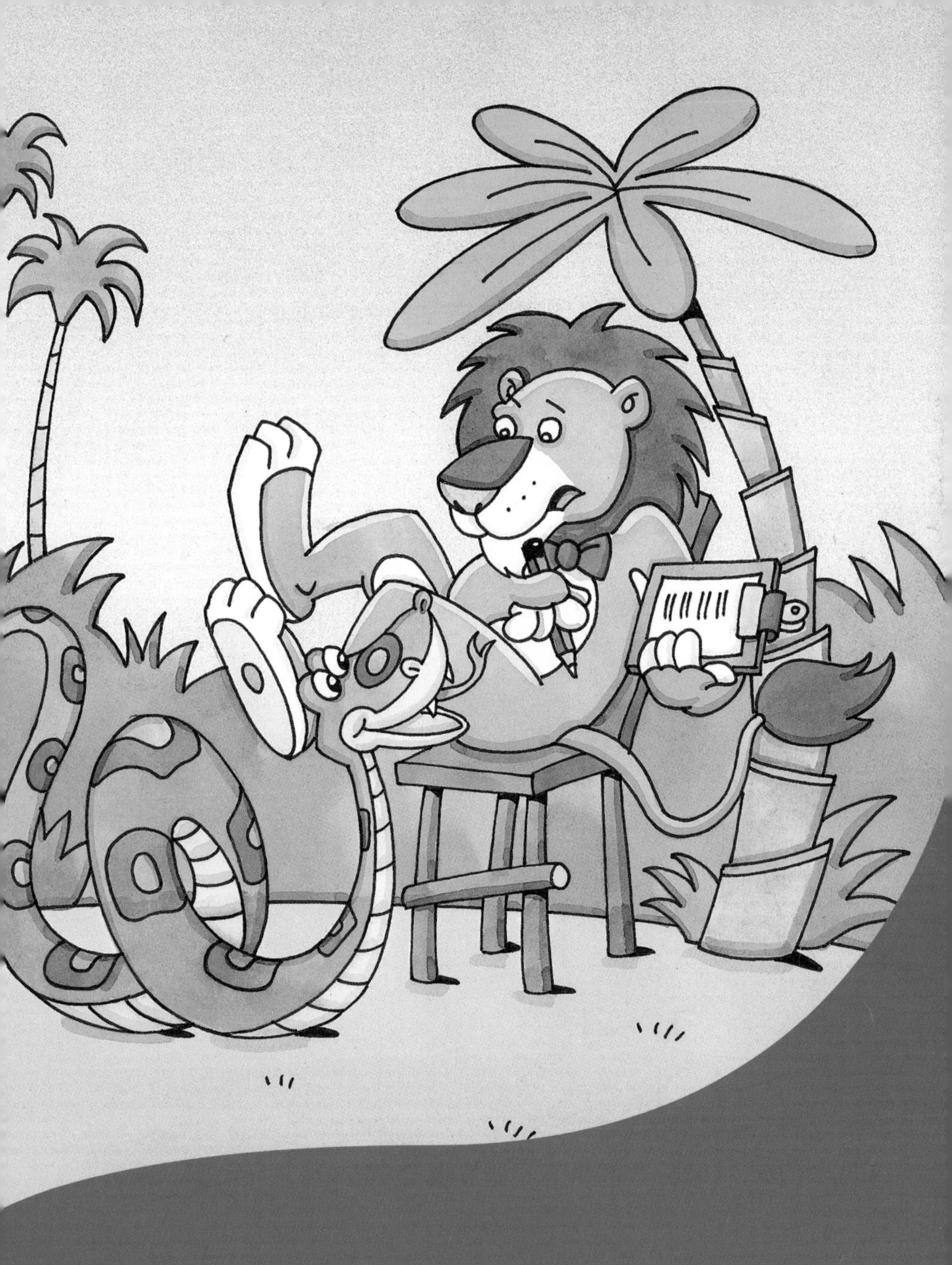

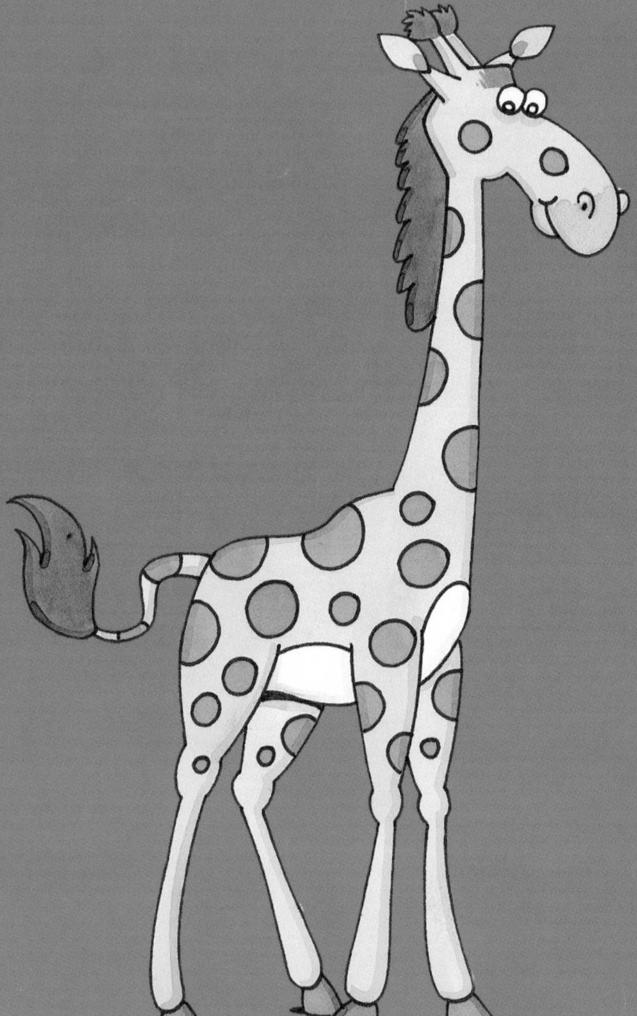

Here is a giraffe.

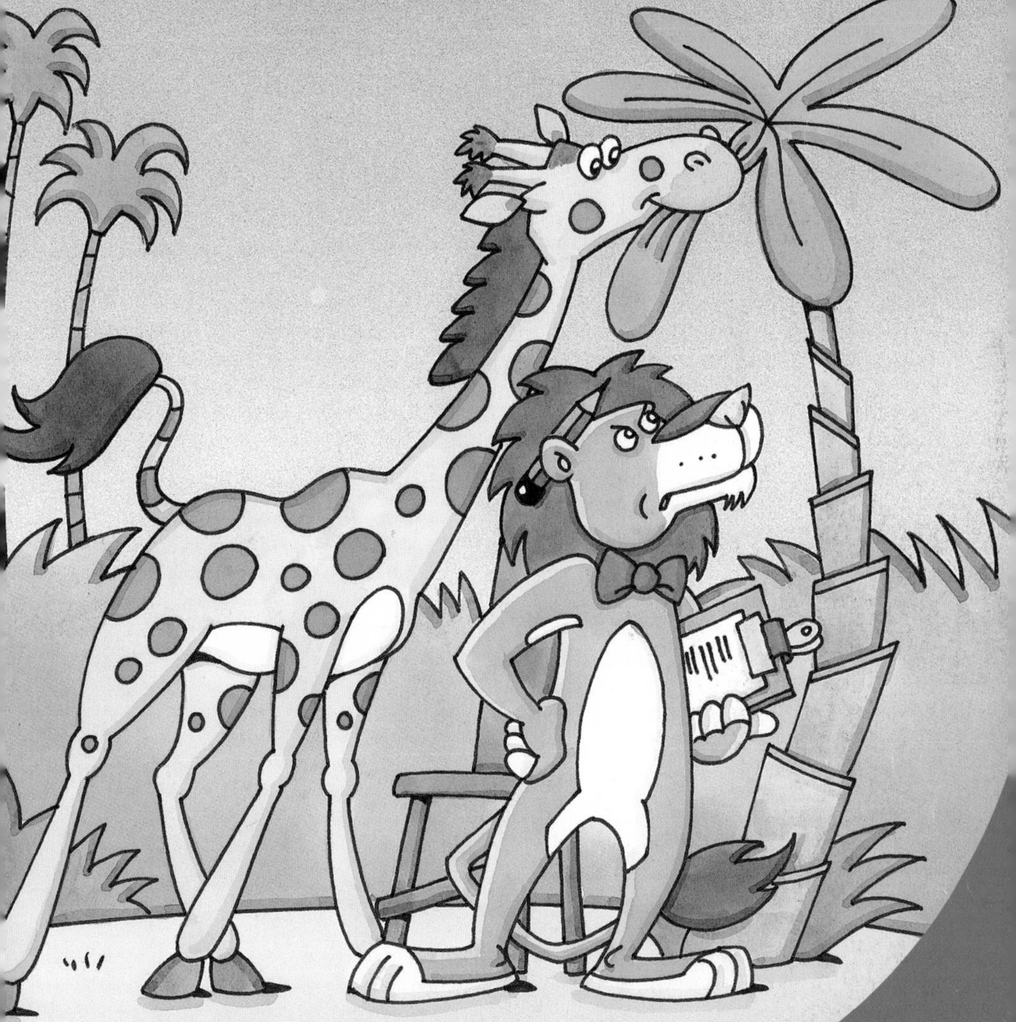

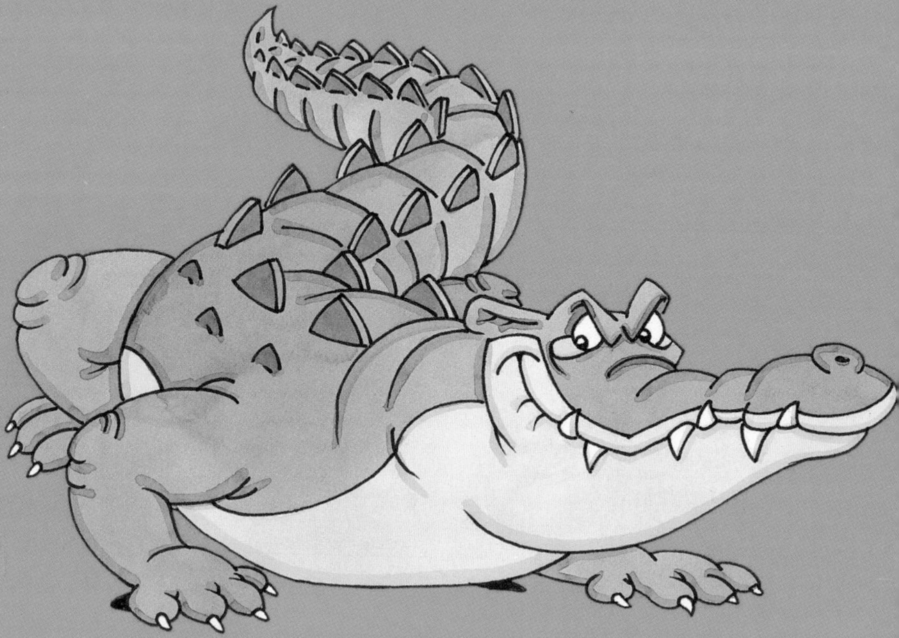

Here is a crocodile.

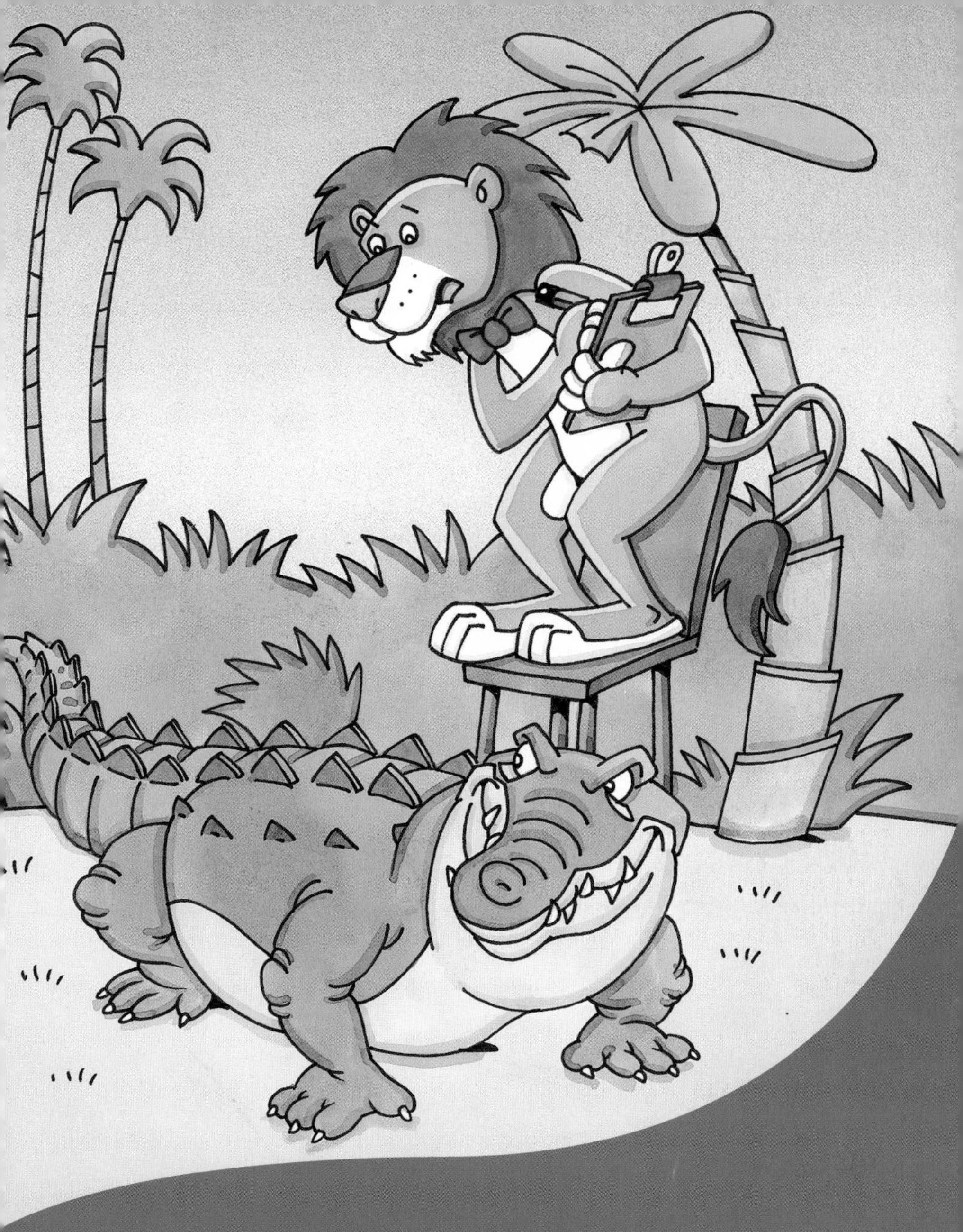

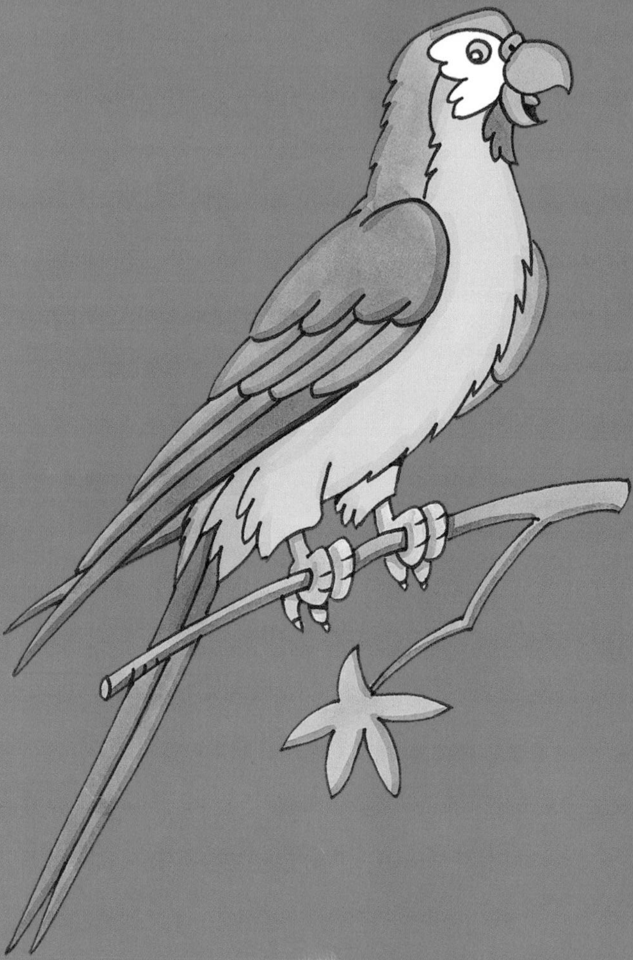

Here is a bird.

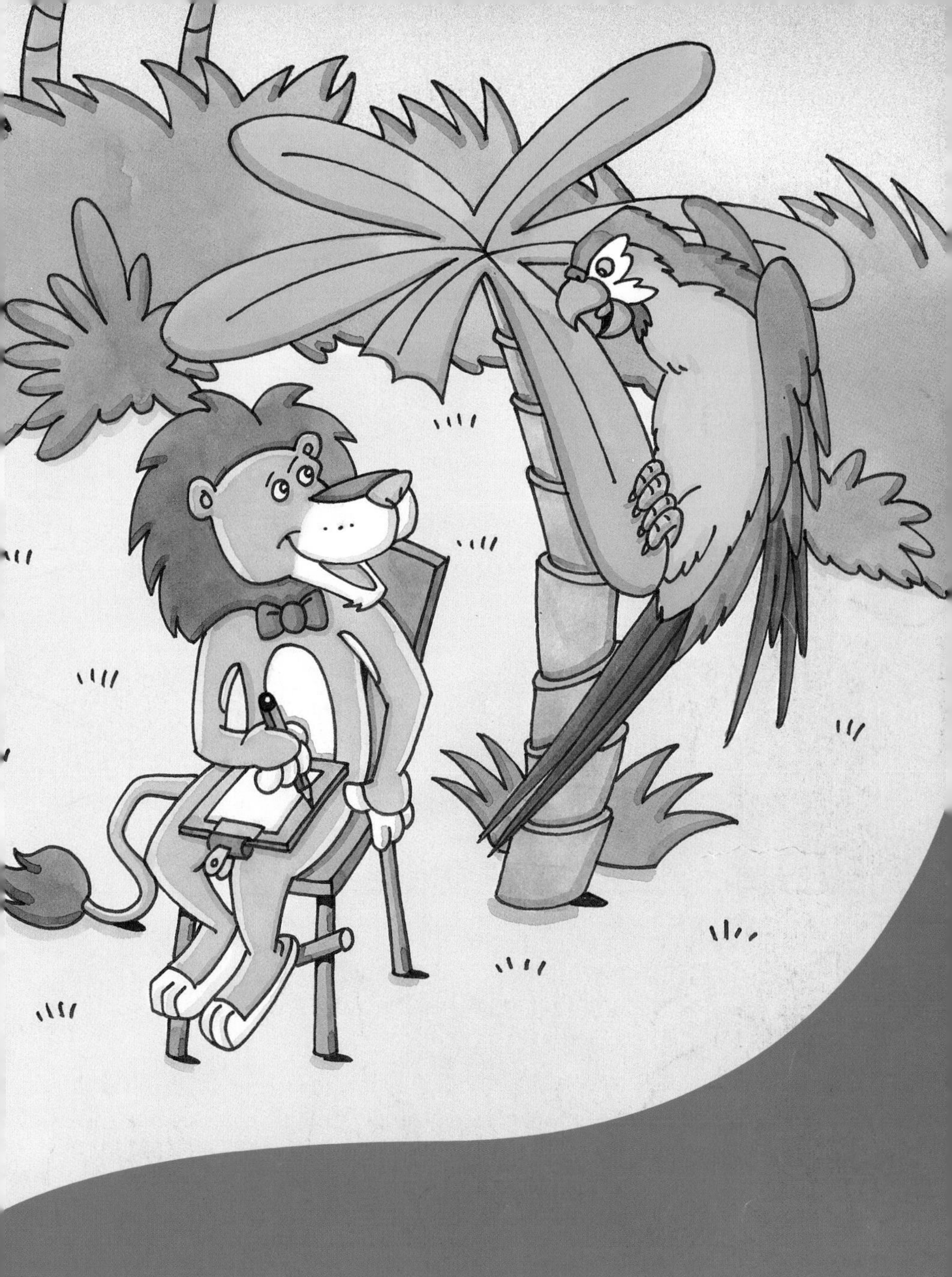

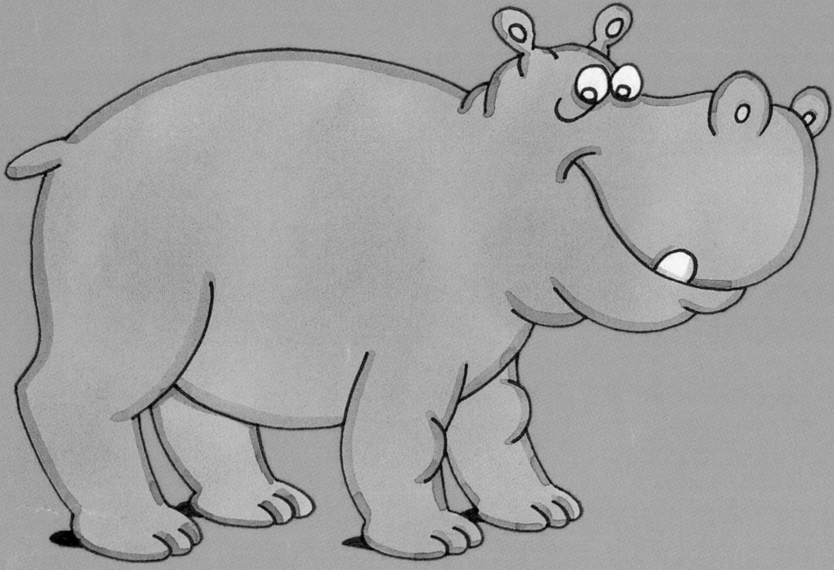

Here is a hippo.

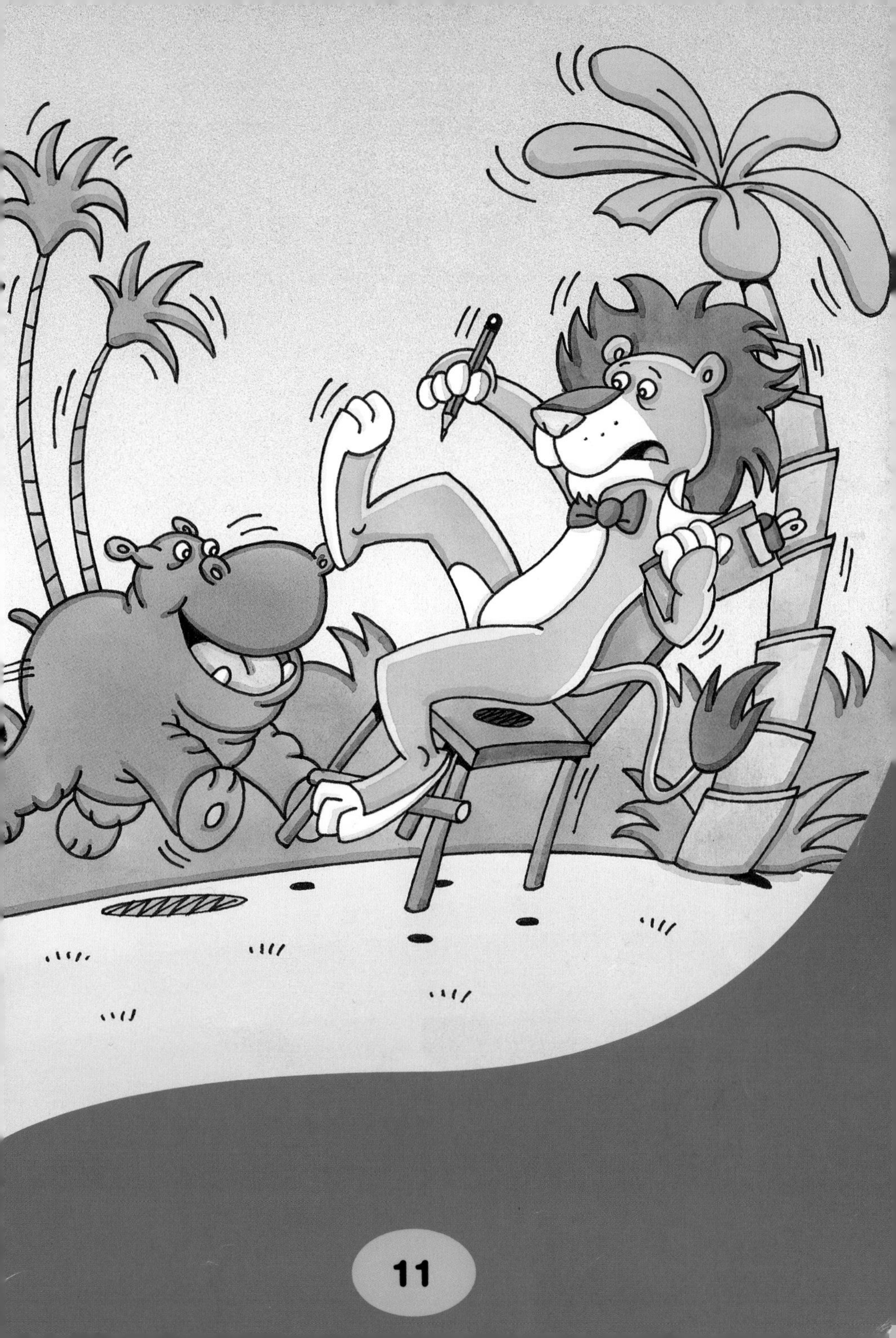

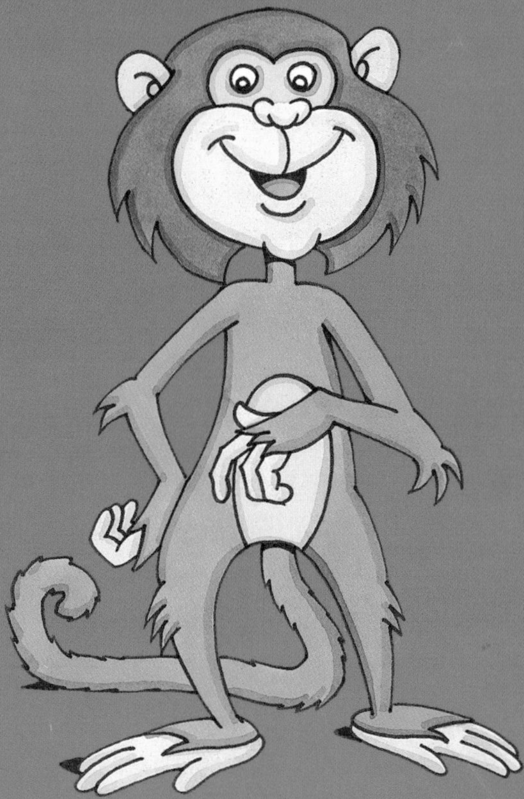

Here is a monkey.